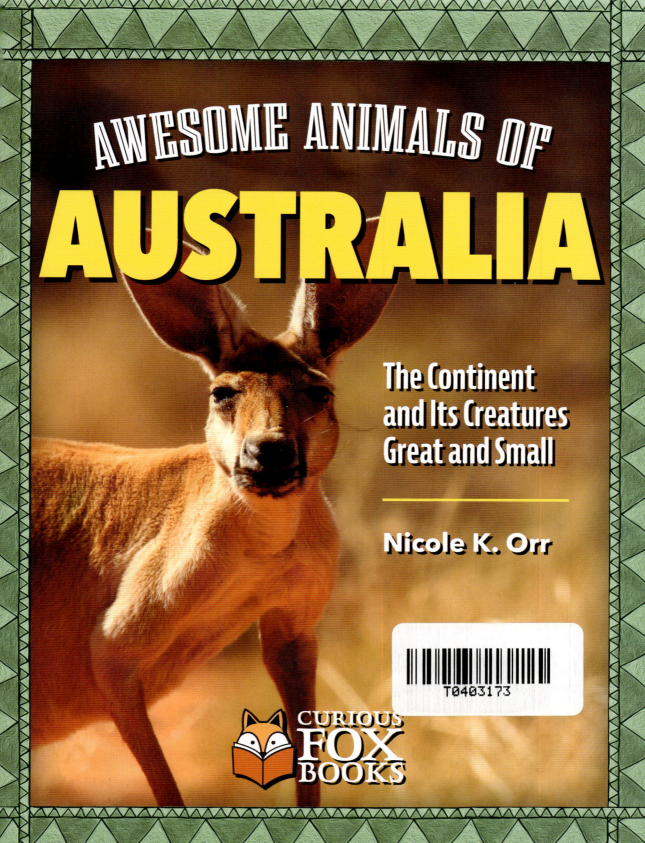

AWESOME ANIMALS OF AUSTRALIA

The Continent and Its Creatures Great and Small

Nicole K. Orr

Curious Fox Books

The different colors on this map show where the mountains are. Light yellow means pretty flat, but orange is very tall!

Welcome to Australia, the largest island in the world! The seasons here are opposite of those in North America. When it is summer in North America, it is winter in Australia.

Much of Australia is made up of desert, called the Outback. This means almost all Australians live on the coast where it is cooler. But it does snow in the southern parts of the country during winter. Australia's biomes range from the Outback's desert to the rainforest on the coast. In the north lies the grassy savanna.

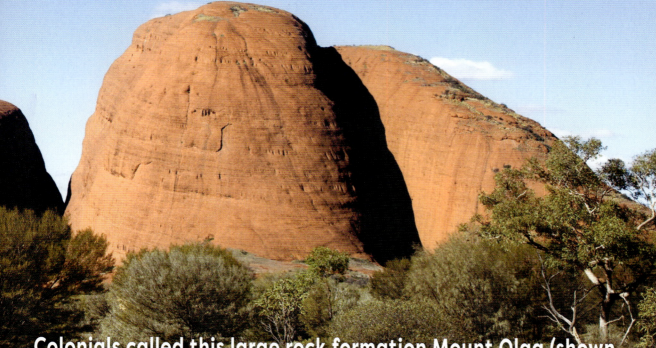

Colonials called this large rock formation Mount Olga (shown here). It is surrounded by sand. Aboriginals call this place Kata Tjuta (KAH-tah CHOR-tah), which means "many heads." Aboriginals have lived in Australia for thousands of years.

The red kangaroo has strong legs and large feet, and it can hop at 35 miles (56 kilometers) per hour. Mother kangaroos have a pouch for carrying joeys (baby kangaroos). Joeys will play-fight with their mothers.

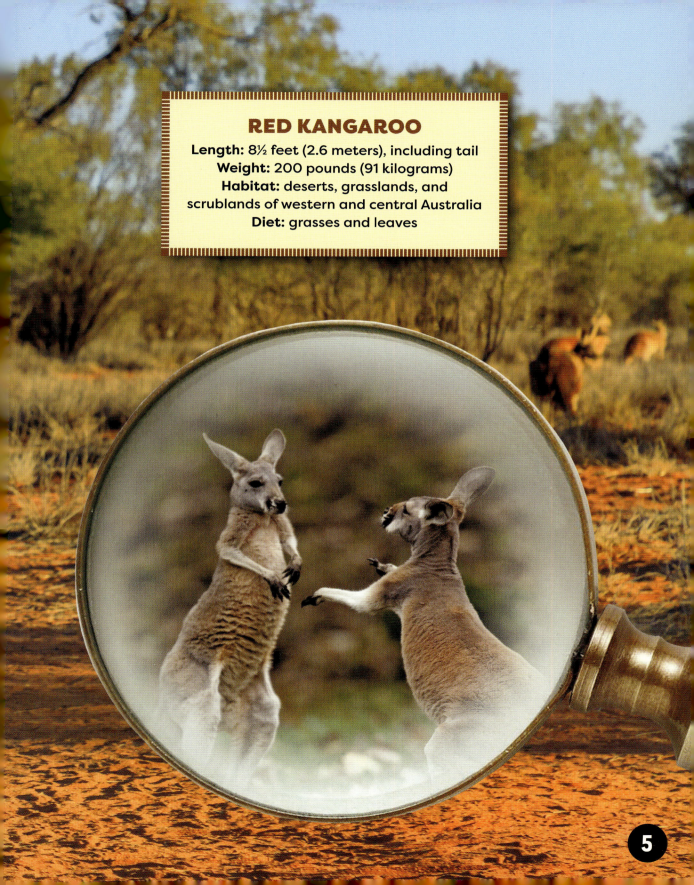

RED KANGAROO

Length: 8½ feet (2.6 meters), including tail
Weight: 200 pounds (91 kilograms)
Habitat: deserts, grasslands, and scrublands of western and central Australia
Diet: grasses and leaves

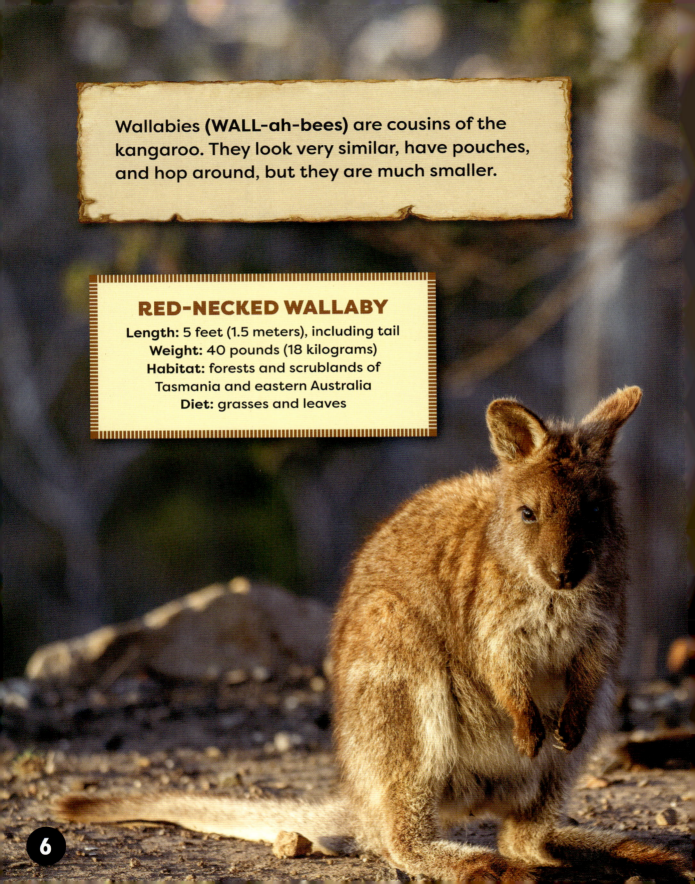

Wallabies **(WALL-ah-bees)** are cousins of the kangaroo. They look very similar, have pouches, and hop around, but they are much smaller.

RED-NECKED WALLABY

Length: 5 feet (1.5 meters), including tail
Weight: 40 pounds (18 kilograms)
Habitat: forests and scrublands of Tasmania and eastern Australia
Diet: grasses and leaves

SUGAR GLIDER

Length: 12 inches (31 centimeters), not including tail
Weight: 5 ounces (140 grams)
Habitat: forests of northern, eastern, and southern Australia
Diet: fruits, lizards, and birds

The sugar glider is active at night. It spreads its limbs to glide through the treetops. Thin webs of skin stretch from its ankles to its wrists are what keep the animal overhead. Sugar gliders can "fly" the width of a football field. They look very similar to flying squirrels, but they are different animals.

Koalas live in small groups in eucalyptus (yoo-kuh-LIP-tus) trees. They will sometimes sleep for 20 hours a day. Koalas are marsupials (mar-SOO-peealz). This means a baby koala will live in its mother's pouch for six weeks.

KOALA

Height: 33 inches (84 centimeters)
Weight: 33 pounds (15 kilograms)
Habitat: forests of eastern and southeastern Australia
Diet: eucalyptus leaves

The quokka (KWA-kah) is known for its smile! Most quokkas live on Rottnest (RAHT-nest) Island, where they have no natural predators.

QUOKKA

Length: 33 inches (84 centimeters), including tail
Weight: 11 pounds (5 kilograms)
Habitat: wetlands and forests of southwestern Australia
Diet: grasses and leaves

The Tasmanian (taz-MAY-nee-an) devil also lives on a small island off Australia. It is called a devil because, when this marsupial gets angry, it will bare its teeth, shriek, and lunge.

TASMANIAN DEVIL

Length: 3 feet (91 centimeters), including tail
Weight: 26 pounds (12 kilograms)
Habitat: dry forests of Tasmania
Diet: small mammals, birds, insects, and fruit

The platypus's snout looks like a duck's bill, and its tail is like a beaver's. A platypus is a mammal. Unlike most mammals, it lays eggs. A platypus holds its breath while it dives underwater. The male holds venom in the sharp spurs on his hind legs, which are used for protection.

PLATYPUS
Length: 2 feet (62 centimeters), including tail
Weight: 6 pounds (2.7 kilograms)
Habitat: rivers, ponds, and streams of Tasmania and eastern and southern Australia
Diet: worms, insects, and shrimp

AUSTRALIAN MAGPIE
Wingspan: 33½ inches (84 centimeters)
Weight: 12 ounces (340 grams)
Habitat: forests and grasslands of Australia and Tasmania
Diet: insects

Bike riders and mail carriers have to watch out for the Australian magpie. The male magpie will dive at humans who come too close to the nest. They are trying to protect their chicks.

AUSTRALIAN WHITE IBIS
Wingspan: 49 inches (124 centimeters)
Weight: 5½ pounds (2.5 kilograms)
Habitat: wetlands of northern, eastern, and southern Australia
Diet: frogs, fish, and crayfish

The Australian white ibis (EYE-bis) has a long, curved beak about 6½ inches (16.5 centimeters) long. They do not have feathers on their heads or necks.

15

CASSOWARY
Height: 6 feet (1.8 meters)
Weight: 187 pounds (85 kilograms)
Habitat: rainforests of northeastern Australia
Diet: fruits

The cassowary (CAS-ah-wayr-ee) cannot fly, but it sure can run—up to 30 miles (48 kilometers) per hour. The fastest a human has ever run is still slower than this! The "horn" on a cassowary's head is called a casque (CASK).

LAUGHING KOOKABURRA

Wingspan: 26 inches (66 centimeters)
Weight: 16 ounces (454 grams)
Habitat: forests of eastern Australia
Diet: insects, worms, snakes, and mice

Laughing kookaburras (KOOK-ah-bur-ahz) will wake the woods at sunrise with their loud calls, which sound like laughter. A kookaburra's beak can be 4 inches (10 centimeters) long.

MANDARINFISH

Length: 3 inches (7.6 centimeters)
Habitat: coral reefs of Pacific Ocean
Diet: shrimps, worms, and fish eggs

GREEN SEA TURTLE

Length: 4 feet (1.2 meters)
Weight: 440 pounds (200 pounds)
Habitat: warm waters of Pacific, Indian, and Atlantic Oceans
Diet: algae, sea grasses, fish, and worms

BOX JELLYFISH
Length: 11 feet (3.4 meters)
Weight: 4½ pounds (2 kilograms)
Habitat: tropical waters of Pacific and Indian Oceans
Diet: fish, worms, and crabs

Just off the northeast coast of Australia is the Great Barrier Reef. It its the world's largest coral reef. The corals provide food and shelter for many animals, including the green sea turtle and the brightly colored mandarinfish (**MAN-duh-rin-fish**).

The box jellyfish is the most dangerous jellyfish in the world with its stinging tentacles (**TEN-tih-kulz**). The box jellyfish is almost invisible when underwater.

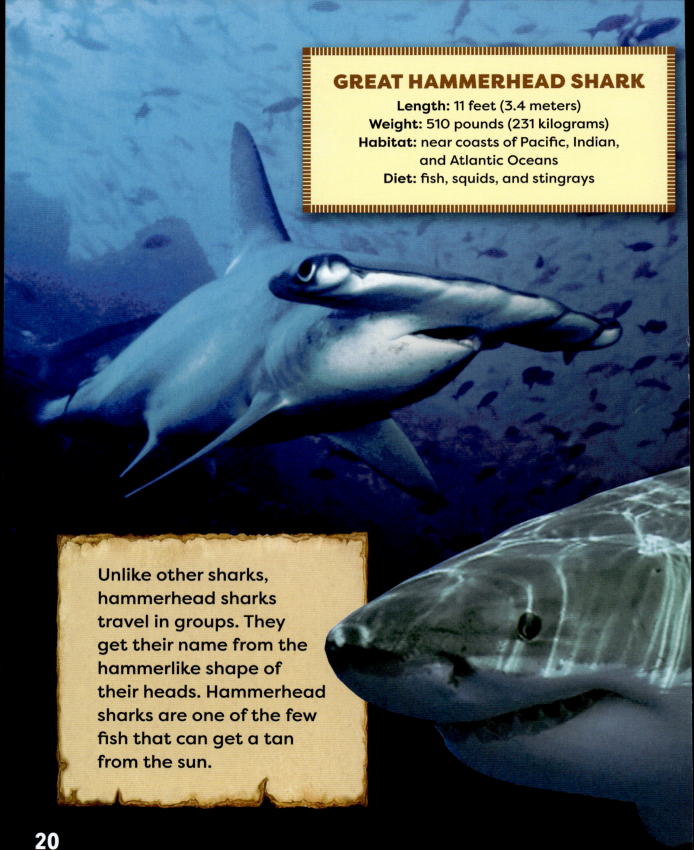

GREAT HAMMERHEAD SHARK
Length: 11 feet (3.4 meters)
Weight: 510 pounds (231 kilograms)
Habitat: near coasts of Pacific, Indian, and Atlantic Oceans
Diet: fish, squids, and stingrays

Unlike other sharks, hammerhead sharks travel in groups. They get their name from the hammerlike shape of their heads. Hammerhead sharks are one of the few fish that can get a tan from the sun.

Great white sharks are so dangerous, they are at the very top of the ocean's food chain. This means they can eat everything else, but they are not eaten by other animals. Their noses can smell blood from ⅓ mile (536 meters) away.

GREAT WHITE SHARK

Length: 19 feet (5.8 meters)
Weight: 4,000 pounds (1,814 kilograms)
Habitat: near coasts of Pacific, Indian, and Atlantic Oceans
Diet: fish, dolphins, seals, and turtles

SALTWATER CROCODILE

Length: 20 feet (6 meters), including tail
Weight: 2,000 pounds (900 kilograms)
Habitat: swamps, rivers, and ocean of northern Australia
Diet: birds, fish, and medium or large mammals

FRESHWATER CROCODILE
Length: 10 feet (3 meters), including tail
Weight: 220 pounds (100 kilograms)
Habitat: wetlands of northern Australia
Diet: insects, crabs, and small mammals

Another creature that lurks in the wetlands of Australia is the crocodile. Its jaws are very powerful, but it cannot chew its prey. It must swallow it whole. Saltwater crocodiles have the strongest bite of all animals.

The inland taipan (TY-pan) is the most venomous snake in the world. This snake lives in the remote deserts of Australia. It escapes the heat by staying in the cracks of dried soil and in animal burrows.

INLAND TAIPAN

Length: 8 feet (2.4 meters)
Weight: 4½ pounds (2 kilograms)
Habitat: deserts of central Australia
Diet: small mammals and birds

Meanwhile, the Australian green tree frog is a friendly animal. It's a common sight in houses and will eat the insects it finds. Australian green tree frogs have waxy skin to keep them from drying out.

AUSTRALIAN GREEN TREE FROG
Length: 4½ inches (11.4 centimeters)
Weight: 4 ounces (113 grams)
Habitat: rainforests of northern and eastern Australia
Diet: insects, spiders, and small frogs

25

The Sydney funnel-web spider is venomous, and it is one of the deadliest spiders on the planet. These spiders mostly stay inside their underground homes. They come out only to hunt. Australia also has some of the largest insects in the world. The adult Hercules **(HER-kyoo-leez)** moth lives just two weeks. When frightened, the Goliath **(guh-LY-ith)** stick insect will open its wings and hiss.

SYDNEY FUNNEL-WEB SPIDER

Length: 2 inches (5.1 centimeters)
Weight: 140 milligrams
Habitat: grasslands of southeastern Australia
Diet: insects and small reptiles

HERCULES MOTH
Wingspan: 12 inches (31 centimeters)
Weight: 1 ounce (29 grams)
Habitat: rainforests of northeastern Australia
Diet: leaves, as a caterpillar; nothing, as an adult

GOLIATH STICK INSECT
Length: 8 inches (20 centimeters)
Weight: 2 ounces (57 grams)
Habitat: rainforests of eastern Australia
Diet: leaves

Wombats (WAHM-batz) waddle when they walk just like penguins do. Believe it or not, a wombat's poop is square.
Dingoes are part of the dog family, but they rarely bark like dogs. They usually howl or growl. A dingo will bury extra food to save it for later.

DINGO
Length: 5 feet (1.5 meters), including tail
Weight: 53 pounds (24 kilograms)
Habitat: deserts, scrublands, and grasslands of central Australia
Diet: mammals, lizards, and fish

COMMON WOMBAT
Length: 40 inches (1 meter)
Weight: 77 pounds (35 kilograms)
Habitat: grasslands and forests of Tasmania and southeastern Australia
Diet: grasses, roots, and barks

Whether you are swimming on the Great Barrier Reef or hiking in the Australian bush, this continent has much to offer.

FURTHER READING

Books

Hirsch, Rebecca Eileen. *Australia.* New York, NY: Scholastic, 2012.
Friedman, Mel. *Australia and Oceania.* New York, NY: Children's Press, 2009.
Olson, Nathan. *Australia in Colors.* North Mankato, MN: Capstone Press, 2008.
Scillian, Devin. *D is for Down Under: An Australia Alphabet.* Ann Arbor, MI: Sleeping Bear Press. 2010.

Websites

Activity Village: Australian Animals
   http://www.activityvillage.co.uk/australian-animals
National Geographic Kids: Australia
   https://kids.nationalgeographic.com/geography/countries/article/australia
Australia: Guide to Australia's Animals
   http://www.australia.com/en-us/facts/australias-animals.html

GLOSSARY

algae (AL-jee)—Simple plants that do not have roots, stems, leaves, or flowers. They generally live in water, in large groups.
biome (BY-ohm)—Any major region that has a specific climate and supports specific animals and plants.
eucalyptus (yoo-kuh-LIP-tus)—Evergreen trees that are mostly found in Australia.
Great Barrier Reef—The largest coral reef in the world. It is in the Coral Sea off the northeastern coast of Australia.
lunge (luhnj)—A sudden forward movement.
marsupial (mar-SOO-pee-al)—Any of the mammals with pouches for carrying their babies.
savanna (suh-VAN-uh)—A flat grassland in a tropical area.
Tasmanian (taz-MAY-nee-an)—A person or animal who lives on the island Tasmania, south of Australia.
venom (VEN-um)—Poison inserted into the body instead of eaten.

PHOTO CREDITS

Inside front cover—Shutterstock/ruboart; p. 1—Shutterstock/Chris Watson; pp. 2-3—Shutterstock/Vibe Images; p. 2 (world map)—Shutterstock/Maxger; p. 2 (country map)—Thomas Steiner; pp. 4-5—Shutterstock/Benny Marty; p. 5 (inset)—Scott Calleja; pp. 6-7—Shutterstock/Wirestock Creators; p. 7 (inset)—Shutterstock/KAMONRAT; pp. 8-9—Benjamin444; p. 9 (inset)—Shutterstock/John Carnemolla; pp. 10-11—Shutterstock/Martin Pelanek; p.11 (Tasmanian devil)—Travis; p. 12 (inset)—Shutterstock/Martin Pelanek; pp. 12-13—Shutterstock/Campbell Jones; p. 14 (magpie)—Shutterstock/Ken Griffiths; pp. 14-15—Shutterstock/Jonathan Steinbeck; pp. 16-17—Shutterstock/Jakub Maculewicz; p. 17 (kookaburra)—Shutterstock/Nicole Patience; p. 18 (mandarinfish)—Shutterstock/Anastasia Mangindaan; p. 18 (turtle)—Shutterstock/Sakis Lazarides; pp. 18-19—Kyle Taylor; p. 19 (jellyfish)—Guido Gautsch; pp. 20-21 (hammerhead)—Barry Peters; pp. 20-21 (great white)—Terry Gross; pp. 22-23—Bernard DuPont; p. 23 (inset)—Shutterstock/aeonWAVE; pp. 24-25—Shutterstock/Ken Griffiths; p. 25 (tree frog)—Shutterstock/Kiki vera yasmina; p. 26 (spider)—Shutterstock/Ken Griffiths; pp. 26-27—Shutterstock/Leah-Anne Thompson; p. 27 (moth)—Shutterstock/Tatevosian Yana; p. 27 (goliath stick insect)—Chris Watson; Shutterstock/pp. 28-29—Shutterstock/puyalroyo; p. 29 (wombat)—JJ Harrison, Caccamo; inside back cover—Shutterstock/ruboart.

All other photos—Public Domain. Every measure has been taken to find all copyright holders of material used in this book. In the event any mistakes or omissions have happened within, attempts to correct them will be made in future editions of the book.

CHECK OUT THE OTHER BOOKS IN THE AWESOME ANIMALS SERIES

Awesome Animals of Africa
Awesome Animals of Antarctica
Awesome Animals of Asia
Awesome Animals of Europe and the United Kingdom
Awesome Animals of North America
Awesome Animals of South America

© 2024 by Curious Fox Books™, an imprint of Fox Chapel Publishing Company, Inc., 903 Square Street, Mount Joy, PA 17552.

Awesome Animals of Australia is a revision of *The Animals of Australia*, published in 2017 by Purple Toad Publishing, Inc. Reproduction of its contents is strictly prohibited without written permission from the rights holder.

Paperback ISBN 979-8-89094-101-5
Hardcover ISBN 979-8-89094-102-2

Library of Congress Control Number: 2024933087

To learn more about the other great books from Fox Chapel Publishing, or to find a retailer near you, call toll-free 800-457-9112 or visit us at *www.FoxChapelPublishing.com*.

We are always looking for talented authors. To submit an idea, please send a brief inquiry to acquisitions@foxchapelpublishing.com.

Fox Chapel Publishing makes every effort to use environmentally friendly paper for printing.

Printed in China